The Adventures of Rizzie Muffin Monster

by
Rhiannon Smith

Dedicated to:

To my Mom and my sister, Shay.
Thanks for always believing in me.
And to K.
Thank you for teaching me how to love.
Unconditionally.

The Human, Riz and Baby Kitty all wake up, ready to start the day.

The Human is singing to the cats:

"Good morning my fluffy babies! Good morning my baby bean toes!"

All three walk into the kitchen.

The Human asks, "Who's hungry?

What would you guys like?

Chicken? Tuna? Salmon?"

Riz turns to Baby Kitty and asks
why the Human never listens to
his muffin requests.

The Human exclaims, "Chicken
it is! Great choice guys, much to
Riz's disgust."

The Human tells the cats as she leaves for work not to have any crazy parties because there was cat litter and catnip everywhere last time.

Riz turns to Baby Kitty and asks him what he wants to do.

Without hesitation he replies, "Cat, Cat, Moose!"

"Alright, Baby Kitty, assemble the animals and let's get this party started!"

Baby Kitty goes first, gleefully yelling "cat" as he taps each stuffed animal on the head and yells moose.

When he gets to Mr. Brownie Bear he is disappointed when Mr. Brownie Bear doesn't move.

Here, let me show you how it's done, BK, says Riz.

Riz slinks around the circle, tapping each stuffed animal on the head and shouting moose when he gets to Baby Kitty.

Riz chases Baby Kitty around the room like a wild moose.

Their fun is interrupted by Mama Bunty, mother to baby bunties, Puff Puff and Sassafras.

"Riz! Baby Kitty! Have you seen my babies? They were digging holes in the Human's garden and now I cannot find them anywhere."

"Have no fear, Rizzie Muffin Monster and Kitty Baby Man are here!! Come, BK, to the magic litterbox we go!" exclaimed Riz.

Riz and Baby Kitty hop into the magic litterbox.

The litterbox spins and shakes, with bright light and cat litter shooting out in all directions.

After the dust settles, Rizzie Muffin Monster and Kitty Baby Man emerge ready to save the day!

Riz and Baby Kitty are looking for clues around the holes the bunties were digging in the Human's garden.

"Riz, I really don't see anything," says Kitty Baby Man.

Just then Mr. Mongoosey, the tap dancing mongoose, strolls by.

"What are you two crazy cats up to?" asks Mr. Mongoosey.

"We are looking for Puff Puff and Sassafras, have you seen them?"

"Maybe I have, maybe I haven't…" replies Mr. Mongoosey.

"You must first have a mini dance party with me before I'll tell you anything further," says Mr. Mongoosey.

The two cats and mongoose begin to dance as if there's no tomorrow. After 20 minutes, Riz asks Mr. Mongoosey where the baby bunties are.

"Oh, I don't know," Mr. Mongoosey replies, "I just wanted to see your sweet cat moves!"

Rizzie Muffin Monster and Kitty Baby Man are left to search for clues on their own as Mr. Mongoosey leaves for his dance recital.

"Riz, I'm not really seeing..." "Shhhh," exclaims Rizzie, turning his satellite dish ears towards the mountains. "Don't you hear that?" asks Riz. "It sounds like baby bunties laughing! But isn't that where the coyotays live? asks Kitty Baby Man. "Yes!" replies Rizzie. "Come on Kitty Baby Man, to the Meow Mobile we go!" exclaims Rizzie.

Rizzie Muffin Monster and Kitty Baby Man hop into the Meow Mobile.

After a couple of attempts, the engine finally starts and they head towards the mountains.

"Kitty Baby Man, stop touching the radio! I said no more techno music and I meant it!" exclaimed Rizzie Muffin Monster.

Rizzie Muffin Monster and Kitty Baby Man rush to the coyotays' lair to find the baby bunties swimming in a saltwater carrot-flavored pool that is warming over a fire.

"Puff Puff, Sassafras, where have you been? Your mother has been worried sick about you, says Kitty Baby Man.

"Kitty Baby Man, what's the pralem? The coyotays invited us for a swim in their pool," replies Puff Puff.

Rizzie Muffin Monster stares blankly and informs the bunties that it is time to go home.

"Not so fast. The bunties are staying for dinner," says Calvin, the lead coyotay.

"Why I oughta give you a poo poo paw to the face!" exclaims Rizzie Muffin Monster.

"No, no, no, big bro. Paws, no claws," says Kitty Baby Man.

"Paw Battle it is! 1, 2, 3, 4, I declare a paw war. 5, 6, 7, 8, try to keep your claws straight!"

Rizzie Muffin Monster and Calvin lock paws in an intense battle of the fur.

The paw war wages on but Calvin is no match for Rizzie Muffin Monster's cat-literal reflexes.

"Winner, winner! The baby bunties aren't staying for dinner, Boom cat!" exclaims Kitty Baby Man.

Rizzie Muffin Monster and Kitty Baby Man whisk Puff Puff and Sassafras home to their Mom safely, just in time to see their Human pull into the driveway.

"Whew! What a day!", says an exhausted Kitty Baby Man.

"Ah, no big deal. Just saving bunties and checking coyotays," replies Rizzie Muffin Monster.

The Human picks up the two
undercover superheroes and asks
if they are hungry.

"Listen lady, I've had a long day
and I just want some muffins…"

Rhiannon grew up in Northwest Missouri, traveling and living all over North America before settling in the West. She has a degree in Business Administration with a focus in Marketing.

Rhiannon has dedicated a large portion of her life and time to volunteer and service work. She has spent time with domestic violence shelters and cat rescue programs. Both of her cats were adopted through a rescue environment and Rhiannon feels very passionately about giving back to the things that are most important to her.

Her aim is to bring laughter and humor through her storytelling. She gets inspiration from her experiences, her nieces and nephews and her animals. Rhiannon lives in Scottsdale with her two cats Ray-Ray and Baby Cat.

Adventures of Rizzie Muffin Monster
Rhiannon Smith

Publisher: MBK Enterprises, LLC/Spotlight Publishing

Printed in the USA

ISBN-13: 9781732072701
ISBN-10: 1732072701

Designed and edited by: Becky Norwood and J Bruce Jones

Cover Design by Angie Alaya / pro_ebookcovers

Cover Photography by: Goran Pesic Goxart

Illustrations by: Goran Pesic Goxart goxart@gmail.com
IS

I was inspired to write this story after going through a rough patch. I was looking into franchise opportunities and felt as though those ventures didn't align with my creative heart and that's when I came up with this silly story.

The characters are based on my cats and I used a lot of the same verbiage in the book is used with my cats on a daily basis.

RayRay was rescued from the side of the road in New Orleans almost 9 years ago when he was just two weeks old. I bottle-fed him and we've been together ever since.

Baby Kitty was added to the mix 6 years ago when I adopted him from the rescue group that I volunteered with, Kitty City Kansas.

Made in the USA
San Bernardino, CA
12 June 2018